A Cow on the Line

and Other Thomas the Tank Engine Stories

Based on *The Railway Series* by the Rev. W. Awdry

Photographs by David Mitton and Terry Permane
for Britt Allcroft's production of
Thomas the Tank Engine and Friends

A Random House PICTUREBACK®

Random House 🏠 New York

Thomas the Tank Engine & Friends A BRITT ALLCROFT COMPANY PRODUCTION Based on *The Railway Series* by the Rev W Awdry. Copyright © Gullane (Thomas) LLC 1992. Photographs © Gullane (Thomas) Limited 1986. All rights reserved under International and Pan-American Copyright Conventions. Published in the United States by Random House, Inc., New York, and simultaneously in Canada by Random House of Canada Limited, Toronto.
www.randomhouse.com/kids   www.thomasthetankengine.com
Library of Congress Cataloging-in-Publication Data: A Cow on the line and other Thomas the tank engine stories / photographs by David Mitton and Terry Permane for Britt Allcroft's production of Thomas the tank engine and friends. p. cm. –
(A Random House pictureback) "Based on The Railway series by the Rev. W. Awdry." Summary: Sir Topham Hatt's engines discover that respect for the rules and for each other pays off in the end. ISBN 0-679-81977-0 (pbk.) — ISBN 0-679-91977-5 (lib. bdg.)
[1. Railroads—Trains—Fiction. 2. Behavior—Fiction.] I. Mitton, David, ill. II. Permane, Terry, ill. III. Awdry, W. Railway series. IV. Thomas the tank engine and friends.PZ7.C83456 1992 [E]—dc20 91-21706
Printed in the United States of America   March 1992   48 47 46 45 44 43
PICTUREBACK, RANDOM HOUSE and colophon, and PLEASE READ TO ME and colophon are registered trademarks of Random House, Inc.

Double Trouble

It was a beautiful morning on the Island of Sodor.
Thomas the Tank Engine's blue paint sparkled in the sunshine as he puffed happily along his branch line with Annie and Clarabel.

He was feeling very
pleased with himself.

"Hello, Thomas," whistled Percy. "You look splendid!"

"Yes, indeed," boasted Thomas. "Blue is the only proper color for
an engine."

"Oh, I don't know. I like my brown paint," said Toby.

"I've always been green. I wouldn't want to be any other color,
either," added Percy.

"Well, well, anyway," huffed Thomas, "blue is the only color for
a—for a Really Useful Engine. Everyone knows that."

Percy said no more. He just grinned at Toby.

Later, Thomas was resting when Percy arrived. A large hopper was loading his freight cars full of coal.

Thomas was still being cheeky. "Careful," he warned. "Watch out with those silly cars."

"Go on. Go on," muttered the cars.

"And by the way," went on Thomas. "Those buffers don't look very safe to me—"

The last load poured down.

"Help, help!" cried Thomas.
"Get me out!"

Percy was worried, but he couldn't
help laughing. Thomas's smart blue
paint was covered in coal dust from
smoke box to bunker.

"Ha, ha!" chuckled Percy. "You
don't look Really Useful now,
Thomas. You look really disgraceful."

"I'm not disgraceful," choked
Thomas. "You did that on purpose.
Get me out!"

It took so long to clean Thomas that he wasn't in time for his next train. Toby had to take Annie and Clarabel.

"Poor Thomas," whispered Annie to Clarabel. They were most upset.

Thomas was grumpy in the shed that night.

Toby thought it a great joke, but Percy was cross with Thomas for thinking he had made his paint dirty on purpose. "Fancy a Really Useful Blue Engine like Thomas becoming a disgrace to Sir Topham Hatt's railway."

Next day Thomas was feeling more cheerful as he watched Percy bring his cars from the junction. The cars were heavy, and Percy was tired.

"Have a drink," said his driver. "Then you'll feel better."

The water column stood at the end of the siding with the unsafe buffers.

Suddenly, Percy found that he couldn't stop. The buffers didn't stop him either. "Ooh," wailed Percy. "Help!" The buffers were broken, and Percy was wheel deep in coal.

It was time for Thomas to leave. He had seen everything. "Now Percy has learned his lesson too," he chuckled to himself.

That night the two engines made up their quarrel.

"I didn't cause your accident on purpose, Thomas," whispered Percy. "You do know that, don't you?"

"Of course," replied Thomas. "And I'm sorry I teased you. Your green paint looks splendid again too. In future, we'll both be more careful of coal."

A Cow on the Line

Edward was getting old. His bearings were worn, and he clanked as he puffed along. He was taking empty cattle cars to a market town.

The sun shone, birds sang, but Edward was heading for trouble.

"Come on. Come on," he puffed.

"Oh! Oh! Oh! Oh!" screamed the cars.

Edward puffed and clanked. The cars rattled and screamed.

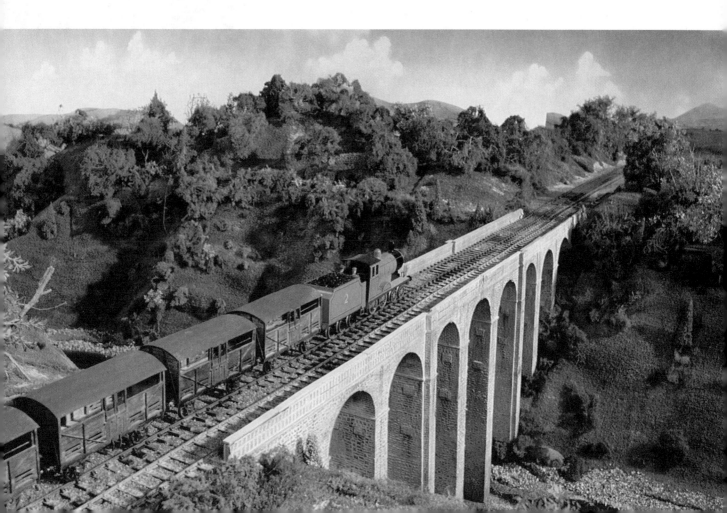

Some cows were grazing nearby. They were not used to trains. The noise and smoke disturbed them.

As Edward clanked by, they broke through the fence and ran across the line. A coupling was broken, and some cars were left behind.

Edward felt a jerk but didn't take much notice. He was used to cattle cars.

"Bother those cars," he thought. "Why can't they come quietly!" He was at the next station before either he or his driver realized what had happened.

When Gordon and Henry heard about the accident, they laughed and boasted. "Fancy allowing cows to break his train. They wouldn't dare do that to us. We'd show them!"

Old Toby was cross. "You couldn't help it, Edward. They've never met cows. I have, and I know the trouble they are."

Some days later Gordon rushed through Edward's station. "Poop, poop! Mind the cows! Hurry, hurry, hurry," puffed Gordon.

"Don't make such a fuss. Don't make such a fuss," grumbled his coaches.

A long stretch of line lay ahead. In the distance was a bridge. It seemed to Gordon that there was something on the bridge. His driver thought so too.

"Whoa, Gordon!" he said, and shut off steam.

"Pooh!" said Gordon. "It's only a cow! SHOO! SHOO!"

He moved slowly onto the bridge, but the cow wouldn't "shoo."

She had lost her calf and felt lonely. "Moo!" she said sadly. Everyone tried to send her away, but she wouldn't go.

Henry arrived. "What's this? A cow! I'll soon settle her. Be off! Be off!"

"Moo!" said the cow.

Henry backed away nervously. "I don't want to hurt her."

At the next station, Henry's conductor told them about the cow and warned the signalman that the line was blocked.

"That must be Bluebell," said the porter. "Her calf is here, looking for her mother. Percy will take her along."

At the bridge, Bluebell was very pleased to see her calf again, and the porter led them away.

"Not a word. Keep it dark," whispered Gordon and Henry to each other. They felt rather silly. But the story soon spread.

"Well, well, well," chuckled Edward. "Two big engines afraid of a cow."

"Afraid? Rubbish!" said Gordon. "We didn't want the poor thing to hurt herself by running up against us. We stopped so as not to excite her. You see what I mean, my dear Edward."

"Yes, Gordon," said Edward.

Gordon felt somehow that Edward saw only too well!

Old Iron

One day James had to wait at the station till Edward and his train came in. This made him cross. "Late again!"

Edward laughed, and James fumed away.

After James had finished his work, he went back to the yard and puffed onto the turntable.

He was still feeling very bad tempered. "Edward is impossible," he grumbled to the others. "He clanks about like a lot of old iron, and he is so slow he makes us wait!"

Thomas and Percy were indignant. "Old iron? Slow? Why, Edward could beat you in a race any day!"

"Really!" said James. "I should like to see him do it!"

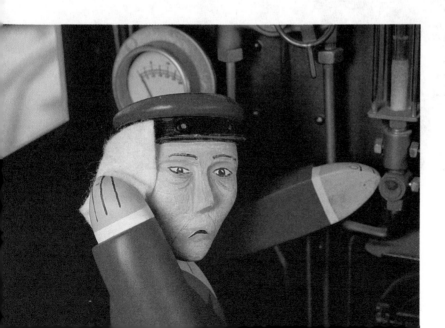

Next morning James's driver was suddenly taken ill. He could hardly stand, so the fireman uncoupled James ready for shunting.

James was impatient.
Suddenly the signalman shouted. There was James puffing away down the line.

"All traffic halted," he announced at last. Then he told the fireman what had happened.

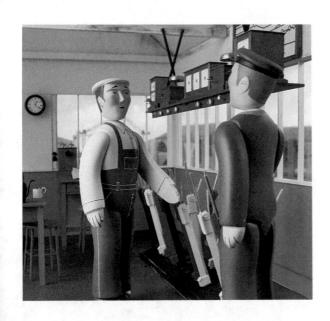

"Two boys were on James's footplate fiddling with the controls."

"Phew!"

"They tumbled off and ran when James started."

Brriinngg!

The signalman answered the telephone. "Yes...He's here...Right. I'll tell him.

"The inspector's coming at once. He wants a shunter's pole and a coil of wire rope."

"What for?" wondered the fireman.

"Search me! But you'd better get them quickly."

The fireman was ready when Edward arrived. The inspector saw the pole and the rope. "Good man. Jump in."

"We'll catch him, we'll catch him,"
puffed Edward.

James was laughing.

"What a lark! What a lark!" He
chuckled to himself.

Suddenly he was going faster and faster.
He realized that he had no driver! "What
shall I do? I can't stop! Help! Help!"

"We're coming! We're coming!"
called Edward.

Edward was panting up behind with
every ounce of steam he had. At last he
caught up with James.

"Steady, Edward!" called his driver.

The inspector stood on Edward's front, holding a noose of rope in the crook of the shunter's pole. He was trying to slip it over James's buffer. The engines swayed and lurched.

At last! "Got him!" he shouted. He pulled the noose tight.
Gently braking, Edward's driver checked the engine's speed, and James's fireman scrambled across and took control.
"So the 'old iron' caught you after all," chuckled Edward.
"I'm sorry," whispered James. "Thank you for saving me. You were splendid, Edward."

"That's all right," replied Edward.
The engines arrived at the station side by side.

Sir Topham Hatt was waiting. "A fine
piece of work," he said. "James, you can
rest and then take your train. I'm proud of
you, Edward. You shall go to the works
and have your worn parts mended."

"Oh, thank you, sir," said Edward.
"It'll be lovely not to clank."

Percy Takes the Plunge

One day Henry wanted to rest, but Percy was talking to some engines.
He was telling them about the time he had braved bad weather to
help Thomas.

"It was raining hard. Water swirled under my boiler. I couldn't see
where I was going, but I struggled on."

"Oooh, Percy, you are brave."

"Well, it wasn't anything really. Water's nothing to an engine with determination."

"Tell us more, Percy."

"What are you engines doing here?" hissed Henry. "This shed is for Sir Topham Hatt's engines. Go away! Silly things," Henry snorted.

"They're not silly." Percy had been enjoying himself.

"They are silly, and so are you. 'Water's nothing to an engine with determination.' Huh!"

"Anyway," said cheeky Percy, "I'm not afraid of water. I like it."
He ran off to the harbor singing: "Once an engine attached to a train
was afraid of a few drops of rain."

"No one ever lets me forget the time I wouldn't come out of the
tunnel in case the rain spoiled my paint," huffed Henry.

Thomas was looking at a board on the quay.
DANGER!
"We mustn't go past it," he said. "That's orders."
"Why?"

DANGER

ENGINES MUST
NOT PASS THIS
BOARD

"'DANGER' means falling down something," said Thomas. "I went past 'DANGER' once and fell down a mine."

"I can't see a mine," said Percy. He didn't know that the foundations of the quay had sunk. The rails now sloped downward to the sea.

"Stupid board!" said Percy.

Percy made a plan.

One day he whispered to the cars, "Will you give me a bump when we get to the quay?"

The cars had never been asked to bump an engine before. They giggled and chattered about it.

"Driver doesn't know my plan," chuckled Percy.

"On! On! On!" laughed the cars.

Percy thought they were helping. "I'll pretend to stop at the station, but the cars will push me past the board. Then I'll make them stop. I can do that whenever I like."

Every wise engine knows that you cannot trust freight cars.

"Go on! Go on!" they yelled, and bumped Percy's driver and fireman off the footplate.

"Ow!" said Percy, sliding past the board.

Percy was frantic. "That's enough!"

Percy was sunk.

"You are a very disobedient engine."

Percy knew that voice. "Please, sir, get me out, sir, I'm truly sorry, sir."

"No, Percy, we cannot do that till high tide. I hope it will teach you to take care of yourself."

"Yes, sir."

It was dark when they brought floating cranes to rescue Percy. He was too cold and stiff to move by himself.

Next day he was sent to the works on Henry's freight train.

"Well! Well! Well!" chuckled Henry. "Did you like the water?"

"No!"

"I am surprised. You need more determination, Percy. 'Water's nothing to an engine with determination,' you know. Perhaps you will like it better next time."

Percy is quite determined that there won't be a next time!